# MY SCHOOL UNICORN

Silver Dolphin

For Lorelei Elizabeth Dewdney. Welcome to the world! – T. K.

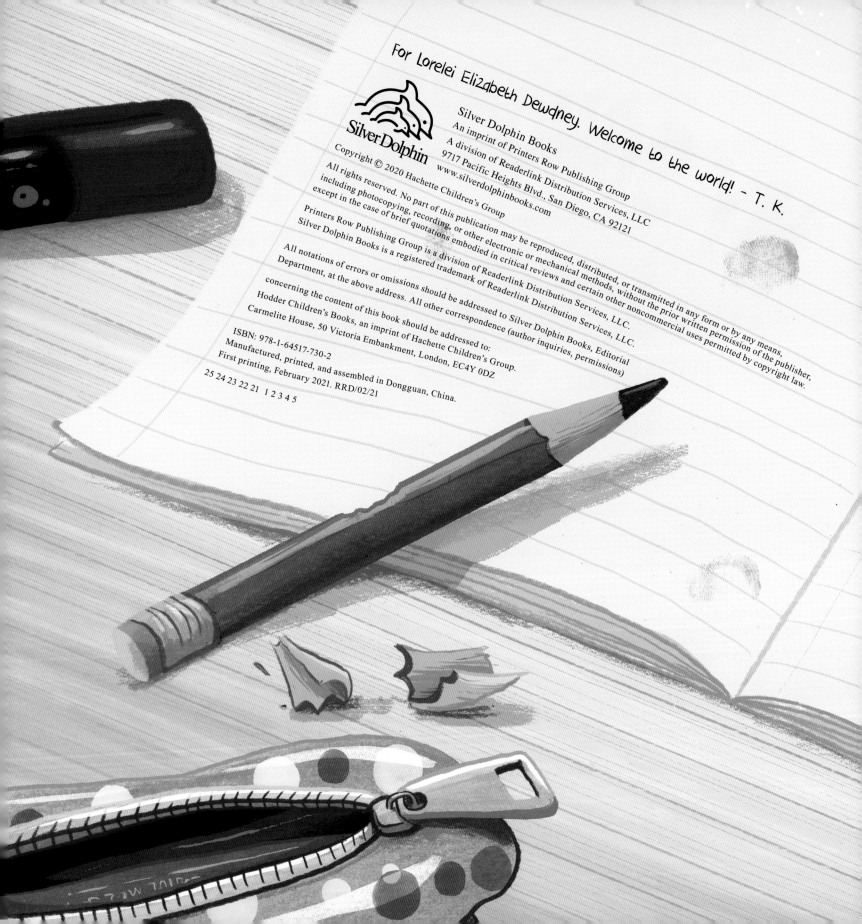

**Silver Dolphin**

Silver Dolphin Books
An imprint of Printers Row Publishing Group
A division of Readerlink Distribution Services, LLC
9717 Pacific Heights Blvd., San Diego, CA 92121
www.silverdolphinbooks.com

Printers Row Publishing Group is a division of Readerlink Distribution Services, LLC.
Silver Dolphin Books is a registered trademark of Readerlink Distribution Services, LLC.

All notations of errors or omissions should be addressed to Silver Dolphin Books, Editorial Department, at the above address. All other correspondence (author inquiries, permissions) concerning the content of this book should be addressed to:
Hodder Children's Books, an imprint of Hachette Children's Group.
Carmelite House, 50 Victoria Embankment, London, EC4Y 0DZ

ISBN: 978-1-64517-730-2

Manufactured, printed, and assembled in Dongguan, China.
First printing, February 2021. RRD/02/21

25 24 23 22 21  1 2 3 4 5

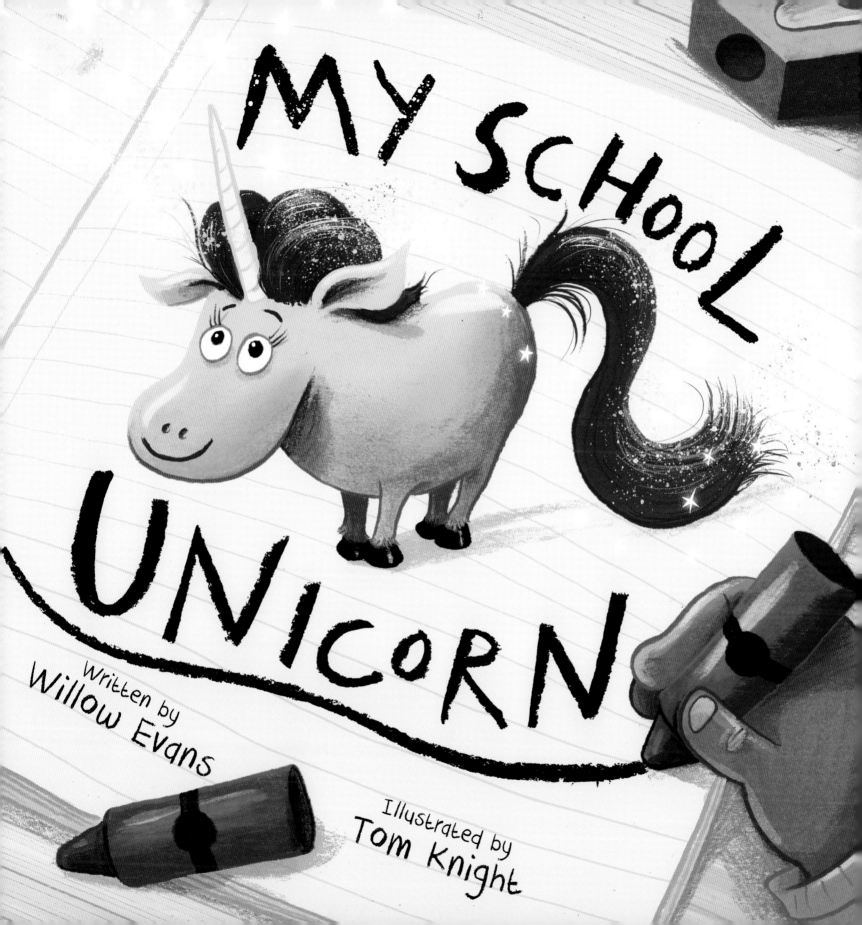

**Evie loved story time with Dad.** It was the very best part of the day.

One night, as Dad tucked Evie in, he said, "Tomorrow is a special day. We're going to pick out your uniform for elementary school!"

Thinking about elementary school made Evie feel all **wobbly**. Preschool was lots of fun, but elementary school sounded scary.

Evie wished that things didn't have to change.

The next day, Evie's wobbly feeling hadn't gone away.
On the bus to the store, her worries **grew and grew.**

"What if I don't make
any friends at school?

What if the lessons are too hard?

What if the lunch is yucky?"

BZT

Tsk BZZZ

CAKE

But then . . .

"Look, Evie, we're here!" cried Dad.

# MADAME LEXI'S

## UNIFORM EMPORIUM

Madame Lexi's Uniform Emporium was brimming from floor to ceiling with **clothes** and **shoes** in every color for every occasion.

SCHOOL

BALLET

SOCCER

KARATE

**"Welcome, Evie,"** smiled Lexi. "Would you like to try on your new school uniform?"

The uniform fit perfectly, but Evie still felt **wobbly.**

"Starting school is a **BIG** adventure," whispered Lexi. "This school unicorn might be just what you need."

"Don't you mean school *uniform?*" asked Evie.

Lexi just winked.

Suddenly, Evie's pocket began to **wiggle** and **jiggle**, and . . .

# PING!

Out popped a **teeny-tiny unicorn.**
His mane sparkled, and his pointy horn
shined with a **shimmering** gold light.

"This is Bobby, your school unicorn,"
whispered Lexi. "Whenever you're worried,
he'll be there to help you feel brave."

"**Wow!**" gasped Evie. Bobby hopped up onto
her shoulder and nuzzled her cheek. The funny,
wobbly feeling began to fade away . . .

That afternoon, Bobby helped Evie get everything ready for her first day at school.

At bedtime, he curled up on a pillow beside Evie's bed. The **shimmering light** from his horn filled the room with a **happy glow.**

The next day, Evie and Dad walked to **school.**

Standing nervously outside the classroom, Evie put her hand in her pocket and felt Bobby give her a **reassuring nuzzle**. Knowing Bobby was there made Evie feel **brave** enough to pick up her bag and wave goodbye to Dad.

The classroom was full of **new faces.**

Evie felt the **wobbly** feeling coming back.
But then Bobby hopped up onto her shoulder.
Evie took a deep breath and picked out an empty chair.

"Hello, I'm Evie," she said. "Can I sit with you?"

"Yes!"
Dylan and
Ava smiled.

Evie spent the rest of the day with her new friends.

With Bobby by her side, new things didn't feel so scary,
and her favorite things seemed even better.

Story time was **magical** . . .

CASTLES

music time was **funny** . . .

playtime was **exciting** . . .

and lunchtime was **yummy!**

The day flew by, and soon it was time to go home.
Evie couldn't wait to tell Dad how fun school had been.

Evie and Bobby went to school together the next day and the day after that. Soon a whole week had passed, and Evie's wobbly feeling had **completely disappeared.**

On Saturday morning, Evie raced downstairs.
**"Is it time to go to school?"**

"No, Evie," laughed Dad. "Today's Saturday.
There's no school today!"

"**Oh!**" Evie had been looking forward to seeing her friends.

"Don't worry, there'll be school on Monday," smiled Dad. "Now, why don't we go to the café for a special treat?"

"**Yes, please!**" cried Evie.

On their way to the café, Dad and
Evie walked past a familiar store.
**Suddenly,** Evie knew what to do.

"Wait here, Dad! I'll only be a minute!"

Dashing into the **Uniform Emporium,** Evie found Lexi arranging the ballet shoes.

DING!

OPEN

"How nice to see you, Evie!
I thought you might be back."

Evie took a deep breath. "I think it's time for Bobby to help someone else. I don't feel scared anymore."

Lexi smiled a **great big, twinkly smile.**

Evie felt all warm inside.

Bobby hopped up onto Evie's shoulder and nuzzled her cheek. Then, with a swish of his tail, he jumped into Lexi's pocket.

Evie smiled. "You were right, Lexi.
**School is a BIG adventure!"**

# HOW TO MAKE YOUR OWN SCHOOL UNICORN

**You will need:**

★ Sturdy paper or cardstock

★ Coloring pens or pencils

★ Scissors (and an adult to help!)

★ Glitter glue is a bonus!

**Step 1.** Place a piece of paper over the unicorn and use your pencil to trace over the lines.

**Step 2.** Use lots of bright colors and glitter glue to decorate your unicorn.

**Step 3.** Ask an adult to carefully cut out your unicorn.

**Step 4.** Pop the unicorn in your pocket and carry it with you whenever you need a friend!